Mirror1

By Kirstie Ruey

Text copyright © 2015 Kirstie D Riley

All Rights Reserved

To those friends that kept my spirits up, I would never have made it without you.

Chapter 1: Perspectives

When you look through a mirror, what do you really see? Is it just an image? Just a reflection? Or could there be something more?

What if the person staring back from inside the mirror is you but at the same time isn't completely the same? A you in an alternate reality where life happened just that little bit differently? Not enough to really notice. A small shift here and there. Things you wouldn't expect to change the future.

How altered could the world be?
How altered could you be?

A young girl smiled at herself in the full length mirror as she got ready for work, her face and mind optimistic for the day ahead. A soft hum permeated the air as she worked, her half asleep brain working quietly away at the thoughts of the day, wondering who she might meet or what she might do. As small town and ordinary as her life was she had yet to say she was really unhappy with it. In her eyes it was comfortable; working behind the register at the local convenience store was an easy was to get money into her pocket and she always had fun chatting to the customers, especially those she had gotten used to. Sure there were bad days, everyone had them, but it was always better to start the day as you meant to go on in her opinion.

She looked at her watch a few moments later, wincing slightly at the time with a muttered curse. It was her turn to open the shop today and it wouldn't do to be late, not that anyone would know about it unless there was a complaint from a customer.

She checked around her room to make sure she hadn't forgotten anything she needed to take with her; counting through the items she had laid out ready for the day the night before, before disappearing from the mirror's view of her small single bedroom.

She smiled as she took one last look around; convinced she hadn't left anything behind before checking her watch again and hurrying out of the door without another glance.

When looking into a mirror, there can sometimes be the nagging need to smile. Maybe it's just a conscious effort to get ready for the day ahead, especially if you know it's going to be a particularly trying one. But what if that's not the only reason? Why is it we smile as if we should be on best behaviour when staring at our own reflections? What if that's actually your subconscious knowing that there isn't just you when you stare into the mirror?

The same girl groaned as she floundered in her bed, growling at the incessant beeping of her alarm before managing to turn it off, almost knocking the clock off its rest in her frustrated attempts to shut it up. Her hand raked through her hair as she stood up, shaking her head in an attempt to wake up quicker, knowing there was little time for a coffee before she made it in to work.

She sighed as she got herself ready for another pointless day at work where nothing interesting ever happened. She wondered what she was doing with her life, working a tedious job at the same dreary convenience store she had worked at since she'd left school. Wondered when she'd get to stop seeing the same people every day and stop having to smile politely and pretend that she was interested in what they had to say and what they were doing with their lives. The pay wasn't even that good and yet here she was, still getting up every day to go to the same dead-end job because there was nothing else for her to do. Because that's what people did after all; they got up, they went about their lives doing jobs they didn't like to get by; it was the way of the world. She knew what people would say if she complained. That at least she had *a job. That at least she wasn't stuck in that loop of job-hunts and interviews and rejection letters that many others her age were in at that very moment.*

She stood herself in front of her mirror once she was dressed in her uniform, making sure she looked as respectful and put-together as everyone expected her to be once she was at work. If they knew what she really thought maybe they'd think differently of her. But then again, we're all only human. We all want something more than what we have.

She smiled at her reflection, using the same fake smile she used for her customers in an attempt to steel herself for what was to come before she stepped away from the mirror, sighing as she checked around her room one last time. She glared at nothing in particular, annoyed that as per usual she was being made to open up the store alone because her manager couldn't be bothered to make the effort.

She walked out of the room at a slow measured pace, not at all concerned about whether she would be late or not. No-one would know anyway.

In a mirror our perspectives of ourselves can be completely different to how others see us. We find the faults in ourselves that sometimes no one else can see.
Conversely in life, our perspectives of other people can be completely different to how others see them or how people see themselves.
Sometimes these perceptions of people can be completely skewed.
It is not always wise to judge a book by its cover.

The girl stared out of the large window at the front of the store, sitting on a small stool behind the counter and swinging her legs, trying not to feel bored at the fact that nobody had come into the store so far. The clock seemed to echo through the store, time dragging slower than it actually was. A book was open before her though she glanced up every few moments, worried someone would snap at her for reading while she should be working even though there was no one there to say anything. She jumped slightly as she heard the whoosh of the automatic doors and the soft tread of someone's boots.

She looked up quickly, taking in the man that had come in through the door - tall, slender but muscular and not much older than herself if she was any good at ageing people on appearance – before her own reflection in the glass beside him made her realise she looked somewhat nervous of him; even if it *was* only from being startled by his entrance. She tried to compose her features into the obligatory smile as the doors closed behind him.

Against her outward appearance, however, the smirk he gave her in return unnerved her.

She took a moment, as he turned away to look at one of the racks, to look him up and down; slightly worried he was a shoplifter. He had a confident aura around him, she noted first; the way he held himself, the self-assured expression on his face. He was dressed all in black leathers, a helmet held under his arm and his hair styled to a point where you knew it must have been expensive. She probably would have been admiring him if it wasn't for the slight nagging worry. Being on her own in the store had never seemed so nerve-wracking and she wasn't even sure why she was feeling this way.

She gulped slightly as he came to the counter, that smirk still plastered on his face as he watched her. Her eyes widened as he leaned in closer when she opened the till to get his change. Her eyes caught her reflection again, seeing the panic in her eyes and his self-satisfied smirk widening when she looked back at him, wondering whether she should slam the till shut quick or not even attempt it. A soft chuckle by her ear made her freeze further.

"You're kind of cute when you're scared."

Sometimes, however, our perceptions are right first time. On these occasions listening to your instincts is not a bad thing.

The girl lounged behind the counter, flicking through the book in front of her with a cursory glance up now and then, not really caring what anyone thought if they came through the door, but still feeling the need to look up every so often just in case. She may hate the job but it would be better to keep it if she could; looking for another would be even more tedious. The automatic doors alerted her that someone had entered and she sat up slightly straighter, more professional, though still trying to act nonchalant. She tensed up, almost an unnoticeable amount, at the man that walked in, warning bells ringing slightly. The guy looked dangerous, a typical bad guy image flicking through her head as she gave him a quick appraisal. Not that she minded the look, he was good looking after all and she felt the need for some excitement in her life. Though she wasn't quite sure this was the excitement she was going for.

She looked back down after a moment, scowling, noticing in her reflection near him that her nervous expression was making him smirk. She mentally shook herself before she looked back up, the fake smile in place as she watched him go around the store. If anyone ever was to ask why, she was keeping an eye on him just in case, using this as an excuse in her head to check him out in relative comfort. She pretended she hadn't been doing just that when he made his way over to the counter, scanning everything through and opening the till without even glancing at him while she worked.

She jumped slightly as she felt the man lean in close to her, looking passed his shoulder at her reflection in the doors, almost as if to check this was really happening and realising, angrily, that once again she looked startled. When she looked back at him, he was smirking yet again at her.

A chuckle near her ear made her shiver slightly, though she tried to hide it as best she could.

"How about you give me all of that?" His eyes focused on the till.

Chapter 2: Similarities

**While sometimes the mirror images outlook on life is different, more often than not aspects of their personality stay the same in either reality.
After all, it is still the same person, right?**

The girl blinked as the man stepped back out of her personal bubble, leaving her with a dilemma. Did she do as he said and hope he'd leave it at that? Or risk his anger and refuse? She once again caught her reflection over his shoulder; pale and tense which incensed her into action as he tapped impatiently on the counter in front of her. She kept the glare on her face, her mouth a thin line as she snapped the till closed, dropping some coins next to his items. "Your change, sir."

The guy stopped smiling, a soft look of shock slackening his face in disbelief before his cocky smile was back, like there had been an unexpected blip in his plan but it was nothing he couldn't handle. "What was that?"

"Your change." She replied coolly before smiling her usual fake smile, her heart hammering in discord to her actions but she felt the need to continue now she'd started. Backing down just wasn't in her nature. "Have a nice day." She left off the customary 'please come again' and with an odd satisfaction, hoped he'd realise that. Her face dropped back into a scowl as he chuckled again. "What?"

"Oh, nothing." He looked up at her, making her heart stutter and her face flush slightly, much to her annoyance. "You've got some misplaced courage there, you know that?"

Her eyes narrowed. "I'll take that as a compliment, now kindly leave."

Instant anger and resistance at being scared for instance.

The girl mouthed the words he had uttered back to herself as the man moved away from her. It felt like it took a moment for them to sink in before a rush of relief went through her as she realised she didn't have to deal with a shoplifter or worse. Two seconds later though, the relieved feeling changed to one of irritation at the man for scaring her like that. She took a moment to rearrange her expression in the window opposite before closing the till and turning back to him, the annoyance showing on her face. "You didn't have to scare me like that you know."

The guy blinked for a second, though a grin reappeared moments later. "It was only a joke, sorry...though it is true."

"What's true?"

He chuckled. "You're cute when you're scared. Well, you're cute in general if I'm honest."

The girl flushed, though she tried to hide it as she put the change on the counter before her. "Your change."

Another similarity could be a persistent nature perhaps.

The girl sighed as she looked up from the counter after hearing the door click open. Once again, the guy she had met before was walking into the shop, like he had every other day since their first meeting, not at all perturbed by her response at the time. In fact it seemed to have made him more curious of her than he would have been otherwise though at least he was no longer trying to rob the store. Her eyes met briefly with her co-worker's, who was trying not to look at him suspiciously, having heard what had happened but at least for the moment she was not alone with him, just in case anything untoward did happen. She was actually starting to find the guy's antics amusing by this point. Who goes to rob a store and ends up buying something from it each day thereafter instead to try and chat to the girl behind the counter?

She turned back to him as he approached the counter, trying to smile as she did with any other customer, taking his shopping and giving him his change without much of an exchange of words. The fake smile froze though when he caught her wrist while it was extended with the change. This was new.

He grinned at her. "So, why don't you come out with me for a bit?"

She blinked at him, confused at the sudden proposal. "Huh?" She shook her head as she realised he was being serious, giving him a disbelieving look as she yanked her arm away. "No thanks. I'm working right now. You know, if you hadn't noticed that fact."

"That's not hard to deal with." He let his arm drop, looking almost disappointed by her pulling away before he walked back to her co-worker. She didn't know what was said. He could have been threatening him for all she knew before he walked back and gave her arm a slight tug again, a smile on his face as if he'd just helped her out. "See? All sorted. Your afternoon is now free."

She spluttered as she was led out, not knowing what to say to excuse herself from this situation, just wanting him to let go of her arm again. There were a million worst case scenarios going through her head but she couldn't quite get her mouth to stop talking. "I don't know a thing about you; I don't even know your name. What makes you think I'm going anywhere with you?"

"It's Gary."

"What?" She looked up at him, shocked she'd even got a response to what felt like her rambling thoughts.

"My name's Gary." He looked down at her, making her realise the height difference and how she had no hope of escape as he put his other arm around her shoulder. She was starting to wish she'd taken

some self-defence lessons. "What's yours?" He grinned as she looked away and mumbled something. "Sorry, didn't catch that."

"Kay."

"Kay?" Gary grinned, relieved that she had been answering him and that he'd finally found out her name, not that it seemed like she was going to notice his reaction any time soon.

"It's short for Katelin but I don't like it, so if you're going to call me anything it'd better be Kay." Kay looked away from him, still trying to appear confident and annoyed at this entire turn of events; even though her heart was beating fast and she was scared stiff of what was going on, she still felt the need to pretend she was fine. It had worked with him before after all.

Gary smiled reassuringly even though she wasn't looking and led her to his bike, throwing her a spare helmet as he let go of her arm.

"You had this all planned out, didn't you?" She raised an eyebrow at him, the helmet shifting between her hands.

He grinned. "Of course, I planned it all. You'd have had excuses to leave otherwise if I hadn't." He sat down on the motorbike, patting the seat behind him. "Come on."

"What makes you think I'm coming?"

"You haven't run away yet." He shrugged, turning away from her, fiddling with his own helmet.

Kay glared at the back of his head, acknowledging his logical approach. She mulled the thoughts over in her head. At this moment she could throw the helmet at him and make a run for it. But then again he did have a motorbike and it wouldn't take him long to catch up. Added to that fact was that she was *kind of curious about where all of this was headed. She looked back at the store, a small smile threatening to tug its way onto her face; he had gotten her away from her boring job for the afternoon. She sighed and sat down behind him, not really knowing herself why she did it, why she didn't at least make an attempt to leave. She stopped for a second once she sat down, not really knowing how to hold on.*

Gary smirked from in front of her, knowing that she couldn't see and again, having thought this might happen beforehand. "You hold here." He reached backwards and caught her hands again, putting them round his waist. His mouth twitching slightly at the sudden tension in the body behind him but he didn't say anything, instead choosing to start the engine. His smile widened as he felt Kay's arms relax into a better position before tightening reflexively as he started up the motorbike.

It took half an hour before he pulled up in front of a shabby looking shack in the middle of nowhere, a sudden awkward tension filling the air as he realised exactly what this might look like and the fact that it was obvious that the girl behind him had gotten intensely suspicious. "So…here we are."

Kay got off the bike, all of her muscles tight with an anxious energy, her entire being wondering why the hell she'd come with him, especially now that she was taking in where she was.

Gary made her jump as he touched her shoulder. He flinched back like he'd been scolded as she skittered away. He raised his arms up in what he hoped was a reassuring gesture. "I'm not going to hurt you, you know."

She shook herself, annoyed that she'd jumped away instead of lashing out. At least then she could have shown him that she wasn't to be trifled with. She gave a short sharp nod before she realised he was going to make her go in first. She shuffled ahead of him, checking back every few seconds to make sure he was keeping some distance between them in the gloom. She blinked as she opened a door ahead of her, the light blinding for a second against the semi-dark corridor.

It took a moment of getting used to before she noticed the other figures sitting around in the room.

Gary smiled at her look of confusion, walking passed her. "Welcome to the Stormchaser's hideout."

Kay looked back up at him, a flash of recognition at the name going through her that had her looking at the group in an entirely different light.

~~~~

Kay looked up expectantly as the door to the store opened with a hum, trying not to smile when she saw it was Gary. He had so far visited every day since their first meeting and she had learnt his name on one of these appearances. Though, she had found out little else from his visits; he liked to ask her questions instead of the other way round and skirted around whatever questions he could without annoying her too much. There was a snort beside her which made her turn with a raised eyebrow. Her co-worker gave her a roll of his eyes that insinuated more than she was ready for. She tried not to blush and glared instead in retaliation, hoping he got the hint to back off. She looked back round quickly as she realised Gary was walking towards her and smiled brightly up at him as he gave her his shopping. On handing back the change to him, he kept hold of her hand.

He smiled at her, hoping he wasn't seeming too forward in anyway. "Hey…would you mind coming with me for a bit?"

"Huh? Now?" Kay stared at him for a moment before realising he meant it. She frowned, she'd have probably met up with him after work if he'd asked but it wasn't like she could just up and leave. "I'm kind of working at the moment?"

Gary nodded and let go of her arm. "OK, give me just a second." He walked over to her co-worker and whispered, grinning when he saw her watching him with thinly veiled curiosity and confusion. She strained to hear them but couldn't make out what was being said and before she knew it he was walking back to her again, still smiling. "Your co-worker said he wouldn't mind if you left for the day." He took her arm again. "Let's go."

Kay followed behind, not really knowing what to say as they walked out and oddly bemused by the entire situation. "Where are we going exactly?"

"Just a little hideaway of mine."

"A hideaway?" Kay looked up at him, a tad worried at this elusive response.

Gary looked down at her, noting the sudden apprehension and almost stuttering in his attempt to reassure. "Don't worry! I'm not taking you somewhere dangerous. My friends just wanted to meet you, that's all."

"And they couldn't wait until after my shift?"

"I thought that you could use an afternoon off."

Kay's amusement at his flustered response increased. She nodded, letting him know she was less worried though more perplexed at the notion. "So…your friends want to meet me? Why?"

Gary's smile reappeared, relieved that she wasn't suspicious of him anymore. "You'll see."

He stepped out from beside her as he reached his motorbike, giving her a helmet.

"You just happened to be carrying a spare?" Kay lifted her eyebrows at him in mock disbelief.

"Of course. I do it all the time." He grinned nonchalantly as he sat down. "You getting on?" He patted behind him.

Kay sighed as she sat behind him, a blush lingering on her face as she realised she had to put her arms around him and she wasn't quite sure whether to just get on with it or not, considering she didn't really know the guy.

~ 13 ~

He took her arms and placed them gently round his waist, tapping them once they were secure, obviously entertained. "You'll fall off if you don't hold on, you know."

"I-I know that."

Gary smiled at the stuttering behind him and the tense grip around his waist as he revved the engine.

Kay looked up when she felt the motorbike stop what felt like only a few moments later but must have been awhile from the twists and turns they took to get there. She noted the shabby building before her with a hint of surprise, her arms slipping from around him as he got up. "This is your hideaway?" She glanced around as Gary stood beside her, helping her off the motorbike, a hand on her shoulder to steady her though he didn't relinquish the grip once she'd got down.

He smiled reassuringly at her as they walked into the hideaway, the gloom as they first entered contrasting the brightness of the next room making it difficult for her eyes to adjust. The first thing she noticed when they did were four other people standing or sitting around the room. She looked up as Gary let go of her shoulder.

"Welcome to our hideaway."

"Who's exactly?" Kay asked, a quiver of confusion entering her voice.

"The Stormchaser's of course."

Kay blinked at him, not understanding at all and wondered if she was meant to know what he was talking about by his cheeky grin.

Chapter 3: Differences

Between realities there are always differences that can be spotted almost instantaneously. Outcomes in the past that have affected the present that never happened in a parallel world. Saying Yes or No to questions that might have once seemed trivial. There are always at least small details that will show up.
No two worlds are ever exactly the same.
Though again, notably, there are always similarities between people and their mirror images.

"Are you trying to intimidate her?"

Kay looked around, staying quiet and observing for now, as one of the men in the room spoke. She made eye contact with him from across the room without even meaning to but he smiled encouragingly at her in response, his mousey brown hair and glasses in her opinion making him look more at home in a classroom, not in some suspicious hideout. She noticed a woman at the same time near the centre of the room; petit but muscular she was sprawled across the sofa and its other occupant, a fair-haired sleepy looking man who seemed to be zoning out of the conversation. She rolled her eyes, shifting in her seat as if bored already with the exchange before going back to a handheld gaming device in her hands.

Gary laughed, an awkward edge to the sound. "What? No, of course not. I'm just letting her know now before she accuses me of not telling her later on."

Kay still stayed quiet, watching the interactions between them, an odd twisted feeling of being shocked by this turn of events and at the same time weirdly unimpressed. So this was the infamous group 'The Stormchasers'? A motorbike gang that was known to roam in her neighbourhood. No one who lived there hadn't heard of them. A group that had a habit of pulling riskier and riskier crimes every time

~ 15 ~

they were sighted. The Stormchaser name suited them; they were thrill seekers pure and simple. She blinked quietly in thought. What had Gary been doing robbing a small store like hers? A fleeting moment of boredom?

"But you have scared her, haven't you? Look how quiet she is." The girl she had noticed earlier sneered at her from across the room.

She bristled at the comment. "I'm not intimidated, just..." She looked over at Gary, an unreadable expression on her face. "I just wasn't expecting it."

"Sure, if you say so." The girl's smirk grew, her comment dripping with sarcasm as she sat up slightly, her game forgotten in favour of the conversation now that there was an interesting party involved. The other occupant of the sofa gave a grumbling noise as she moved, put out by her fidgeting from where she's been leaning against him.

Kay scowled at her before looking away, noting the room's final occupant sitting in another chair further back had yet to say a word. It was hard to analyse much from his appearance; his jittery movements taking most of her attention. He looked like he wanted to ask a million questions but knew better than to voice them right at that moment, which made her wonder what she might be in store for later. She walked into the room properly for the moment, her head held high, to show how unfazed she was of them all. Her mouth ran away with her again as she muttered. "Well, there's not really much to be scared of, now is there?"

"Huh?" The four in front of her blinked in disbelief, eyes glancing to their friend behind her as he grinned, obviously glad that this was her response to them all.

Kay tilted her head at them, scrutinising them. "Well, from what I know you've never hurt anyone in a crime you've committed, now have you? Unless it was an accident that is." She added the last sentence quickly, noticing that she was going to be interrupted. *"You know what I mean; you've never gone out of your way to take people out. You've also never taken jobs purely to hurt people, only heists and robberies."*

"H-how could you possibly know that?" The guy who had spoken first tried to smile but it came across as fake and uncertain.

Kay shrugged. "I like living on my own, people got worried when they found out what neighbourhood I lived in so I found what information I could to make them less worried. I'm just glad I didn't have to lie about it." She smiled at the group; trying not to giggle at the dumbfounded looks they were giving her in response. She turned back to Gary, a smug satisfaction taking over when she saw he looked shocked as well. "Are your friends always like this when you bring girls here? I mean I know there's protective but this little meeting is a little extreme." There was a snort behind her and Gary's ears turned red, glaring behind her at the sniggering girl on the sofa.

"Actually, he's never brought a girl here before." The guy who'd spoken first came forward, his smile a lot more natural and relaxed now. "Sorry if we seemed rude. I'm Ryan." He held his hand out to her, trying to be polite.

"Kay." She took his hand, shaking it.

Ryan nodded before looking round, making his way around the room as he did so. "The one who's being snarky is Moira. I'd say her barks worse than her bite but...I'm not so sure that's true." The girl raised a hand at Kay, eyes already back to her game as she flicked her dark hair out of her way. She flopped once again onto the man beside her, getting a resounding exhale of breath for her efforts before she made herself comfortable resting her head in his lap. "The one she's draped over is James. He's our leader." The man smiled at her and nodded, still as quiet as when she first entered. "And over there in the corner is Liam, he's-."

Kay blinked and suddenly the other man was in front of her, eyes alight with curiosity, cutting off Ryan's introduction. "Hi!" He pulled back slightly when she didn't respond with a small frown. Kay staring at him as he started to speak, not understanding everything he said and pretty sure he got tongue-tied, with the speed he was going at, at least twice. She was only really able to discern 'glad to meet you' and 'hope you're here to stay so we can get to know you' from the mess of questions and ramblings spewing from his mouth.

"Who on earth gave you coffee?" Kay blurted out without meaning to, earning an approving laugh from across the room. She tried to ignore the reproachful look Liam gave her in return.

"Sorry, he gets like this. You should see him on a heist, he's like a whirlwind. You want something done fast, he's your man. He just doesn't know when to slow down." Gary pulled Liam away and ruffled his hair. "I think you've scared her more than anything else has. She definitely wasn't expecting that kind of welcome."

"Technically I wasn't expecting any kind of welcome. I had no idea where we were going or what we were doing." Kay crossed her arms, slightly put out when her remark was ignored.

"I scared her?" Liam looked slightly distraught at even thinking about it.

"He's messing with you, Liam." Ryan spoke over his shoulder as he walked into one of the other rooms. "I'm going to make drinks, come and help me before he teases you further."

"K." Liam darted after him, grin once again set on his face.

Kay walked over to the guys on the couch, fairly amused at the atmosphere, not really having expected this for a gang's hideout, especially one so infamous in the local area. She leaned against the back of the sofa, peeking through the doorway into the next room where Liam was buzzing around Ryan who had an exasperated look on his face as if he wondered why he'd made the effort. "Liam is not what I expected in The Stormchasers."

"Yeah well Ryan keeps him out of trouble and he's good at what he does. If you're wondering they're not together."

"Oh? Why would I have thought that?"

"Lots of people before you have."

Kay looked down at Moira, who shrugged half-heartedly while she spoke, eyes still glued to the screen. Kay smirked at her sprawling figure over the other man. "Do the same questions get asked about you two?"

Moira looked up then for a moment, a mirrored smirk on her face. "Now how would you know that?"

Kay snorted. "Because it's so hard to tell." She chuckled as James coughed and looked away from the pair of them with feigned disinterest.

Moving away from them she hit something hard with her foot and winced, hoping she hadn't broken something. Looking down she sighed with relief at the game box she'd almost stepped on. She tilted her head to read the box a few seconds later as something dawned on her. "Eh? This doesn't come out until next week."

Moira paused the game, shocked at the response. None of the guys they were with had any inkling of what she was playing. She grinned in surprise. "I know right? It's taken so long to come out, I just couldn't resist. Do you want a copy?"

"Ye-" Kay paused, realising what the 'I couldn't resist' probably meant. "Actually, no, it's OK. I think can wait until next week."

"Suit yourself."

Gary smiled from where he leant against the doorway, glad that she seemed to be settling in without a hitch. He hadn't actually let himself hope it would go this smoothly. He was slightly worried about her getting so friendly with Moira so quickly. They had enough trouble dealing with her antics without her having a helper. Deep in this thought he jumped as he realised someone was standing next to him without him even noticing.

Kay grinned, giving him an appraising look. "You may look the part but you sure don't act like you're in a gang."

"So you say but you were terrified of me when we first met." He grinned as she pouted.

"Yeah but if I'd known you were part of the Stormchasers I wouldn't have been actually." She smiled as he looked confused. "Well, what would be the point of robbing a small convenience store? It's not like there's much excitement in that kind of robbery...you must have been looking at something else, now weren't you?" She whistled innocently, hearing the laughter echoing from the other room and sighed softly. What was she doing here? In fact what were any of them doing here? It was weird to know that you were in the hideout of a notorious gang and yet feel less anxious than you had before, even if all the details still eluded you. Then again, she had wished for a more exciting life. "How did you guys get into all this anyway? You hardly seem the types."

Gary shrugged. "We work for a bigger syndicate; they don't mind how we do our jobs as long as we get them done and as long as we don't get caught."

She rolled her eyes. "You know what I mean, don't avoid the question. How did you get involved in the syndicate then?"

Gary shrugged again. "It just kind of...happened? Though it took a little convincing to get these guys involved." He frowned. "I still feel kind of guilty for getting Ryan involved, he was really against it all but when everyone else said they wanted to be a part of it, I think he just came along to make sure we looked after ourselves."

"Oh. Well that was stupidly kind of him."

Gary chuckled, shaking his head at the remark. "I guess it was, maybe if he'd been more decisive we wouldn't have done this."

Kay shrugged. "Maybe or maybe it would have just been the four of you with no one to look after you all."

An echoing 'Oi' came from the other side of the room where Moira had been listening in, made them both laugh.

~~~~

"Oi, Gary, I thought we had got through to you about that stupid name." The girl on the sofa dropped her head back against the other man sitting there with a thud that made him wince. "You're embarrassing us."

Gary laughed. "What? It's not that bad a name and you were all for it before."

"Yeah, when we were how old, exactly?"

Kay looked round the room, smiling back at one of the occupants before looking back and forth between the two bantering. "Sorry." She cleared her throat, interrupting them. "Am I missing something here?"

Gary shrugged. "It was just a name that we came up with, when we were younger, for us lot, when we thought about becoming a gang."

"A gang?"

"Well that doesn't matter now, does it?"

Kay turned to the man who had smiled at her earlier as he crossed his arms, a disapproving look on his face. "Huh?"

The man smiled again though it was strained as he pushed his glasses back up again. "We sorted that out a while ago."

The girl on the sofa snorted again. "You mean you made sure we weren't stupid and turned down the offer before we even had a chance to think it through."

"Yeah, I guess. But you've got to agree, it really *was* a stupid idea. Can you imagine what kind of trouble we'd have got ourselves into by now?" The man turned back from the sofa to Kay, an apologetic look on his face. "Sorry, I haven't introduced us. I'm Ryan-"

"The responsible one of us all. What would we ever do without him?"

Ryan rolling his eyes. "The one who can't stop talking is Moira. That's James she's using as a seat and that's Liam." He pointed behind him to the others. "You're...Kay, right?"

She nodded, smiling slightly. "Is it that hard to remember the names of the girls he brings back?"

Moira let out a burst of laughter and even Ryan couldn't hold back the small smile. "No, that's not it. We've heard a lot about you and I wanted to make sure I got your name right."

"That and Gary has never brought someone back before." Moira smirked at him before going back to her game.

Ryan grinned, unable to resist but decided it would be best to disappear before Gary got annoyed at being laughed at. "I'll go get some drinks."

"See? Told you. Responsible host, isn't he?" Moira winced slightly as Ryan ruffled her hair as he walked passed, shaking her head to get it out of her eyes again with a frustrated grumble.

Kay smiled awkwardly as the last member of their group Liam wandered up to her, not entirely sure how to react to him just yet. "Hi?"

Liam grinned at her, alleviating any uncomfortable atmosphere. "Gary's told us all about you-"

"Only good things I hope." Kay grinned, teasing, though she almost regretted it when he took a step closer."

~ 22 ~

"Of course! He only ever said good things. I hope you stay around- if you like us that is. You sound like a nice person-" He paused as Ryan called for him in the kitchen.

"Go on, Kay's not going to have disappeared by the time you get back." Gary grinned, shaking his head at the obvious dilemma in the other's head.

"K." Liam grinned before running off to follow the shouting.

Kay walked slowly into the room, looking around curiously as she did so. "So, what is this place anyway? You said it was your hideaway but…" She gave a soft grimace of distaste at the old place. "It's not exactly appealing is it?"

Gary shrugged behind her, leaning against the doorframe. "Maybe not, but it's our place and a place no one would come looking for us."

"Looking for you?" Kay tilted her head, confused and suddenly alert.

"He might not have told you but we all come from rich families. You know the 'follow the rules and join the family business' types." Kay turned as Moira spoke, one hand up in a flourish to accentuate her words. "So this place is kind of…where no one would think to come looking for us. Our getaway area I guess."

Kay nodded. "Huh, I can see that." She looked around again, a soft smirk on her face. "Who would think rich boys – and girls would ever be in a place like this." Her smirk widened slightly at the glare she got from Gary but she feigned ignorance and sauntered over to glance over Moira's shoulder at whatever she was playing. Her eyes widened. "That isn't out for a while yet, how did you get this?"

Moira looked up at her, with a small chuckle. "How do you think? Money does wonders after all…you want a copy?"

Kay frowned at the admittance. "No it's fine, I think I can wait."

The other girl shrugged. "If you say so."

Kay turned her observations from the room to its occupants, noting how the two fit together on the seat; how Moira settled back down and without a hint of complaint the guy beneath her shifted to be more comfortable. She quirked an eyebrow, her inquisitiveness getting the better of her. "You two an item or something?"

Moira's face scrunched up at the mere thought. "Uh, No. We're just friends, have been since we were born or something like that. If you want the lovebirds of the group, they're in there." She jerked her head back, motioning towards the door the other two had gone through.

Kay leant backwards to peek through the doorway, smiling as she saw the two on the other side goofing around. They had most definitely forgotten about whatever it was they were actually supposed to be doing, not that it seemed anyone minded at all.

"Though if you do ever meet anyone else we know, which is doubtful, don't say anything about that."

Kay tilted her head slightly, her smile shifting. "Why?"

"No one else knows, and it would be hard for them to tell their parents especially as Liam's are trying to marry him off to some girl so that they can bring the companies together."

"Ahh…that's sad." Kay looked back through the doorway, feeling sorry for the couple. "But they're going to have to say something at some point, right?"

Moira shrugged. "Yeah, we know but when they do is up to them, isn't it?"

"Of course." Kay smiled in what she hoped was a reassuring manner as even the ever quiet James seemed to watch her for the correct answer. She shuffled her way back across the room as the pair seemed to accept this answer and went back to lounging.

Gary looked up as she came close, trying to act nonchalant about everything. "So what do you think? I mean, I know it *is* a bit run down and all…" He pretended to be insulted by her earlier words, sniffing sadly.

Kay laughed brightly. "Yeah, maybe it is. But the company more than makes up for that."

Gary brightened at those words. "You think so?"

Kay nodded. "You've got some good friends here." She smirked, unable to hold back a snarky comment. "But the five of you even contemplating you could be some intimidating gang is beyond me." She cracked up at his indignant look and the small grumble from the couch behind her.

Chapter: 4. Silence

Sound doesn't penetrate mirrors. If you are directly in front of one then lip reading may be possible. But even then there may be a mistranslation across the surface. Therefore an act may look like the same scene is being played out, but the conversation might be entirely different.
Though these conversations and interactions may inevitably lead to the same destination.

Kay frowned as she entered 'the base' as she'd decided to call it not long after her first visit. Moira had come to pick her up from work today, which was unusual to say the least. The girl had shrugged nonchalantly though with a 'thing's had come up unexpectedly' so she hadn't argued. She'd slowly begun to get used to coming here after work, a thing she'd never expected to happen. She'd never expected the invitation to last further than that first day, never thought they'd actually accept her enough that Gary had once again arrived, this time when she finished work, the following day and every day thereafter to pick her up and take her to see them, if only for an hour or so some days. It wasn't just up to them though; they'd made it clear on that first day that if she wanted to leave she could and she wouldn't have to deal with them again but by that point she was intrigued by their lives. The excitement rubbing off on her as she slowly got to know the other members of the Stormchasers over the passing weeks.

She looked around as Moira walked past her and nodded, smiling knowingly as she went over to her usual place on the sofa where, as per usual, she found the comfiest seat on James. Kay had decided Moira was one step ahead of the boys at all time, not that they had any inclining of this. She liked to get her own way, not that Kay could blame her; her ideas, though reckless, were usually innovative and when questioned she'd have already thought steps ahead of them to counteract their arguments. In those cases she would concede if the others pointed out something she hadn't thought of but if it was a usual matter, like one of the other guys testing her patience, she could usually be found putting those inventive skills into pranking them mercilessly instead. Not that Kay had seen too much of this side of her yet but she had been told about a few pranks that had made her crack up. Her laughter growing at the disgruntled faces of the other members as she giggled, obviously agreeing with Moira that it was a suitable punishment.

Her eyes trailed next over James who caught her gaze and nodded at her from his seat as he shifted over slightly for Moira before looking down once again at whatever he was reading. James was the quiet one of the group; the one that seemed like he was slightly out of focus most of the time, which had at first confused Kay, considering he was meant to be their leader. But over the weeks it had become apparent that he was actually listening and observing instead of interacting and so probably knew a lot more than he let on on a normal basis. Watching them plan a mission as they called it had drawn a conclusion to this suspicion when the group turned as one to him to check his input on the 20 minute discussion they'd been having. He'd made it clear that he'd taken all their points into account before weighing up his options and coming up with a plan that incorporated them. Kay smiled, he didn't only pay attention to the situations but came up with a compromise to suit everyone. It had also helped that he'd shocked her by warming up to her a bit on her second visit and remembered enough to spark up a semblance of a conversation even with only a word or two exchanged between them the first time they'd met.

Kay turned, walking towards the kitchen, having nothing better to do and smiled as she came across Liam. Liam was like a breath of fresh air whenever she saw him, always happy to chat about anything and everything. He seemed like he could bounce back from anything and his smile was infectious.

Liam turned as he heard footsteps, his normal grin seeming slightly strained which alerted her that something was wrong instantly. "Hey, you. How you been?"

"You saw me literally yesterday." Kay rolled her eyes in good humour before she frowned at the lack of response. It took a second for her to notice she hadn't seen Ryan or Gary yet and wondered whether that had anything to do with the way Liam was acting. Wondered whether there was more to why Moira had picked her up, with a small nervous pit in her stomach. "Umm, where are-?" She didn't have time to continue before a loud thud echoed from upstairs, along with what sounded like raised voices but she couldn't make out what was being said. She raised an eyebrow, the nervous pit disappearing. "Never mind. I'll hazard a guess they're upstairs."

There was a chuckle behind her the front room and kitchen close enough to talk from room to room from. Moira grinned cattishly from the sofa. "It's harder to hear an argument when it's upstairs. Ryan thought they should have some privacy for this particular one apparently."

Kay hummed thoughtfully. "An argument about what exactly?" The room went almost static with the sudden tense quiet which made her freeze in realisation. "I'll take this silence as they're arguing either has something to do with me or it's something they don't want me to hear...that about cover it?"

"Hmm?" Moira tried to act like she had no idea what she was on about. A feigned innocence settled around the three of them that she wasn't buying.

She scowled as no one actually agreed or contradicted her, still deciding it was best to stay in this awkward limbo. "Fine, either way there's only one thing to do." She walked over to the stairs before they could register what she was up to, deciding that if they were talking about her, she had a right to know. She snuck up quietly, wincing at even the smallest noise the stairs made under her before slipping silently next to the doorframe.

"I can't believe you're honestly thinking about doing this." Kay could hear the angry exasperation in Ryan's voice as he snapped, though he had obviously calmed down enough from whatever Gary had told him to no longer be shouting. That or he'd realised they might be able to hear him downstairs, his voice quiet and waspish.

"Well, I have thought about it. I think it's a good plan." Gary sounded defensive and sulky at the way the other was acting, like he hadn't expected this reaction.

"You're making a mistake, involving her in thi-" Ryan stopped as Liam called from downstairs, much to Kay's annoyance as she knew he'd done it purely to cut her eavesdropping short. "We'll talk about this later, Gary."

"No, we won't. I'm going to tell everyone else now, we don't have much time and you know that." Gary opened the door to find Kay trying to make a hasty retreat downstairs and pretend, unsuccessfully, that she hadn't been listening in. Gary blinked for a few seconds before giving her a smug knowing look, obviously unperturbed by the turn of events. "How long have you been standing out here, Kay?" He saw Ryan stiffen out of the corner of his eye as he walked through the door.

Kay shrugged, hoping she didn't look too guilty. "Not long, only a few minutes. I got worried when I heard shouting, that's all." She looked over Gary's shoulder at Ryan as if concerned for them but just eager to make it appear she hadn't heard anything that had been mentioned. "Is everything OK?"

Gary sighed as Ryan walked past him without saying a word, just a poignant look. "Yeah, everything will be fine."

~~~~

"So, where're the other two hiding?" Kay looked around the living area of the hideout when it was clear two of their number were missing. She'd been confused since Moira turned up at her work but she hadn't felt the need to ask, assuming there must be a reason for it. It wasn't like she minded spending time with Moira or the other two; she got along with them great and was hoping that she was slowly getting to know them better with all the time she'd spent visiting them. She nodded at James in greeting before making her way to the kitchen area, smiling to herself as she heard more than saw Moira flop against him.

"Hey." Liam grinned at her from the kitchen though his eyes kept drifting towards the stairs behind her in obvious annoyed curiosity.

Kay raised an eyebrow at the action. "I was going to ask where Ryan and Gary were again but I'm guessing they're upstairs?"

Liam nodded before shrugging and going back to washing up, sniffing in an offended manner. "Gary asked Ryan for a word about something." He pouted slightly. "I wanna know what they're up to but he said he only wanted to talk to Ryan about whatever it was."

Kay grinned mischievously. "Well then. Should I go find out?" She darted up the stairs hearing a quiet whine behind her from Liam as he tried unsuccessfully to get her to come back down as well as an amused 'go for it' from Moira. She snuck up softly and headed down the first corridor as silently as possible, listening intently. She paused triumphantly at a door as she heard voices coming from inside.

"Are you sure about this?" Ryan's voice sounded intrigued and a tad disbelieving.

Kay froze as she heard a shuffling sound, thinking it was one of them coming towards the door. She gave a relieved exhale when it appeared to be just one of them fidgeting. There was a hint of embarrassment in Gary's voice when he replied. "Yeah, I'm sure. You don't think it's a good idea then?"

"No, no, I think it's a great idea."

Kay tilted her head, her head buzzing with speculations about what they could be talking about before zoning back in with a wince as she moved her foot and made a floorboard groan loudly. She looked up sheepishly as the door opened, knowing she'd been caught red-handed.

"How long have you been there?"

Kay giggled guiltily, her hands fidgeting nervously in front of her. "Not long enough to know what you're talking about unfortunately." She shrugged, knowing that telling the truth was probably better in this situation, even if it bugged her. "Liam was curious, I took the initiative." Her grin faltered as Ryan stiffened and walk straight past her. "Don't be too hard on him, it wasn't his fault he couldn't stop me."

Gary sighed endearingly after his friend. "Don't worry, he'll be fine. Ryan's too nice to actually get mad at him. He'll just scold him for almost ruining it."

"Ruining it?" Kay narrowed her eyes at him when he didn't respond. "So…do I get to know what that was all about?" She trailed after him as he walked down the stairs.

"You'll find out soon enough, don't worry." He smirked, ignoring the rest of her questions.

**The differing conversations can also have an adverse effect on the atmosphere surrounding it.
A picture can paint a thousand words.
But not all of them are necessarily correct.**

The time seemed to trickle past slowly as the four people who weren't privy to the private conversation waited for one of them to actually tell them what had happened. They had tried to slip away from it, the conversations drifting back and forth but each always ended in a pregnant pause as they waited for someone else to fill the void.

The six of them ended up sat in the main living area of the hideout, most of them curiously glancing at Gary who was fidgeting restlessly. He would look up every so often as if he was ready before thinking better of it and shaking his head, glancing away again. Only Ryan was looking impassive throughout all this though he was trying to keep a smile off of his face as far as the others could tell.

"Gary, can you please just tell us what's going on?" Kay sighed as she sat on the floor, her back against the sofa, flicking through a magazine that she'd found in the hopes it would curb her curiosity. It had failed miserably. She tried not to grin as Liam's face lit up or as Moira's eyes flicked over to Gary again even though she was pretending, unsuccessfully, to be more interested in her game again like the first time they'd met.

Gary opened his mouth as if to answer before closing it again with a snap. He turned to James as if trying to stall for time, his smile forced. "Hey, James, do you still have those tickets?"

James frowned before reaching over for his bag and pulling out what Kay could only assume were the tickets Gary was talking about though they looked much more like high class invitations to her. "These?"

Moira snorted as Gary nodded, looking unimpressed at the tickets. "I don't know why they still give us those; it's not like they don't know who we are and that we'll be going regardless."

"It's so we can bring guests." Gary spoke in a rush as if scared he might back out if he didn't say it fast enough.

"Oh." The simultaneous answer from Liam, whose eyes lit up again in understanding and Moira, who smirked as well, made Kay frown.

"Am I missing something here?" She thought she understood but playing clueless, she thought, might give her more answers more quickly. "What are the invitations for?"

"It's a big formal event." Ryan finally joined in the conversation. "It's hosted by our families every year so we always have to go whether or not we want to."

"And I was wondering if you'd come with me." Kay turned slowly to Gary who in turn refused to look at her.

~~~~

Time had a nasty habit of slowing down when an argument had yet to dissipate. That inevitable calm before the storm hit again that had everyone tightly wound up ready for a blow was grating on all of their nerves.

There as an awkward silence amongst the six of them as they loitered in the living area of the base, conversations trying and failing to bring the mood any higher than dismally grey. Kay tried to hide her curiosity along with the others, knowing better than to voice anything with this tension brewing, as they watched Gary fidget restlessly; his eyes darting to Ryan every so often who sat silent and brooding in the corner. His face stayed resolutely impassive but the aura around him seemed heavy with a pulsing anger.

Kay sighed, her fraying nerves showing through as she gave up on the hesitant approach around the pair. "OK, this all needs to stop, seriously. What the hell are you two hiding?" She put her hand up as they started to protest, her face stonily saying she was having none of it. "OK, OK, I'll ask a different question then. What are you two arguing about?" She ignored Liam looking up in sheepish curiosity, and Moira's quick glance before deciding it was much safer to stay out of this particular show.

Gary went to answer, Ryan's gaze behind Kay the only thing that stopped him. He glared in return, turning to James who was watching with a calculated look, obviously connecting the dots about what was going on. "James, have you come up with anything else for our next assignment?"

James shook his head, pulling out some invitations from his bag, playing with them with a thoughtful air. "Not really. It's obvious that we need a diversion and there aren't many we can choose from for this kind of job."

Gary took another hesitant look over at Ryan, who was still trying to keep a lid on his temper, as a small gasp of understanding echoed from one of the other two. "Exactly, we don't have *many options."*

"Right, this is getting us nowhere fast, I'm still in the dark here." She looked between Ryan and Gary, her face dark. "So how about just telling me what exactly is going on and letting me figure out whether I should be a part of it." She let it hang in the air that she had heard more than she'd let on of their conversation upstairs.

Ryan sighed, relaxing slightly when he realised there was no getting out of this now. "We have an assignment that takes place in a week's time. The job we've been given is to rob a hotel while everyone is busy with the big event that is going on upstairs. The event itself is kind of a distraction but relying on that could blow up in our faces.

So we need to create a diversion ourselves, or at least have someone in the event there to warn us if anyone gets alerted to our presence."

Kay could feel what was coming next and didn't know whether to be apprehensive or excited by the prospect. Were they really offering her a chance to be a part of one of their jobs?

"So, we..." Gary rolled his eyes at the sharp glance he got from Ryan for his wording. "I was hoping that you'd help us with this." He looked over at her briefly. "After all, it's much less suspicious to have a dance partner than to go alone to a formal event like this."

Chapter: 5. Reflection

**A reflection in glass can be bleached of colour.
The situations completely different.
The places the same.**

If Kay had been told when she first met the other guy that she'd be going to the most talked about event of the year, she would have laughed in their faces.

As it was, a week after being asked to join them for the festivities, she still felt highly self-conscious of the fact that she was so very below par for such an event.

"A-are you sure I look OK?" Kay shouted from the top of the stairs, walking out of the room that she'd been getting dressed in. She walked down the stairs, waiting for an answer that never came. She was still slightly perturbed at them meeting there of all places just before this big occasion but she thought better than to question it; asking hadn't helped in the past. The group seemed to be less inclined to talk about their home lives and families so after a while she'd just stopped prying. She walked down the last few stairs, tense at the silence ebbing over her from the others. She pulled up the skirt slightly so that she didn't trip over it as she made the last step, glad that whoever it was out of them, she assumed Moira, that had chosen the outfit hadn't decided that she needed to be a few inches taller with the dress trailing the floor like it did. The thought of tripping and ripping a dress that felt like it was worth more than a few months' pay checks, was just one of the possible scenarios that had come to mind in the last week. She gave an awkward twirl at the bottom, the black dress's skirt spinning with her as she played with the small dark red flowers that fanned up its right side. "Well? You're all a bit quiet to be honest. It's not very comforting." She looked sheepishly up at the five in front of her, an odd feeling of envy at the way they held themselves as if it this was an everyday occasion.

"Y-you look great." Gary grinned out of his shock at her.

She rested her hands on her hips, her eyes disbelievingly. "Now why don't I believe that?"

"Because you're being difficult." He held out his arm to her. She took a second to appreciate the white suit adorning him, the red accents complimenting her own outfit though she couldn't tell in that moment. "And you're nervous. You shouldn't be. You look fine."

Kay rolled her eyes and took his arm. "Fine, but if I get funny looks at this party I blame you entirely."

The others chuckled discreetly behind them as the couple jokingly bickered, neither of them noticing that they were watching fondly.

~~~~

What happened next was a week of preparation. A week of going over and over the plan, changing pieces here and there until they all had it down, satisfied that they could pull this latest assignment off.

Now the start of robbery was finally upon them.

Kay licked her lips as she walked down the stairs, adrenaline pumping through her as she realised exactly what she was doing. She tried her best not to slip down the stairs, glad that no one had tried to make her wear high heels otherwise she would have already stumbled and probably toppled down head first. Not the best way to show that you were up for what might be the biggest take of the year. She had at first wondered why she was even needed, but it had become clear that although they would all enter, the others would be slipping away leaving only her and Gary as the lookouts; and if needed, as the distractions. She looked up at the overly dressed group in front of her as she got to the bottom and did a slow twirl, the white dress slipping around her before her hand went nervously to the embroidery of red flowers. The outfit felt heavy but in a good way, grounding her. "What do you think?"

"Perfect." Gary smirked slightly, looking her up and down without a hint of subtlety.

Kay fidgeted slightly, glaring at him teasingly, before noticing Ryan's gaze on her. She sighed. "What is it, Ryan?"

"I still can't believe you agreed to do this."

She rolled her eyes, trying to dispel her nervousness unsuccessfully and ended up shaking her head instead in defeat at him. "Can we not do this, please, Ryan? I'm nervous enough as it is without you joining in."

"Sorry."

Gary glared over his shoulder for a second as he hooked her arm through his and led her out the door before turning back to her and encouraging her as they left.

Sometimes our reflections show us things about ourselves that we really wish we didn't have to see.

Kay stared out of the dark window, her eyes unfocused between the city view and the reflection of herself and the room behind her. The hotel's conference room had an outside wall of complete glass that was one of the reasons the hotel had been chosen to host in the first place. A slight frown marred her face, something about the reflection of the room seeming off but she couldn't put her finger on what it was exactly. She tried to ignore it, zoning back out again; liking the fact that the reflection on her black dress made it look like it was made of the city lights outside. It was why she had stopped and stood there in the first place but that nagging feeling in her head kept forcing itself to the surface no matter how much she tried to crush it. She jumped as she felt someone put a drink in her hand, glad that they steadied it so that she didn't spill it in her moment of clumsiness.

"Didn't we tell you, you looked absolutely fine?" Gary smiled reassuringly at her before taking a sip of his drink.

Kay pouted. "Yeah, yeah, whatever." She looked around the room. "Where are the others anyway?"

Gary shrugged. "Who knows? Ryan said something about him and Liam going somewhere with less prying eyes and James and Moira got bored of the entire affair and decided to go out for some air."

Kay laughed. "They don't like this kind of thing then I take it?"

He smiled back, glad she had relaxed a bit. "No."

"And you?"

"Not usually." He held out his hand, putting both their drinks down on a nearby table. "So…are we going to dance?"

Kay's eyes widened, worried at the shift. "I can't dance, you know. I told you that when you first asked me to come."

Gary, still smiling, pulled her towards the dance floor without any hint of worry. "And? You're beautiful, that's all they'll be talking about when this is all over."

Kay gave a huff of contempt. "Unless, oh, I don't know, I fall over and smack my face on the ground? Or take you down with me. Oh god, that's even wors-"

Gary laughed, cutting off her panicked mutterings before they could go too far. "You'll be fine, I promise. I'll make sure you don't fall over."

Kay grimaced as she was led out on to the dance floor but it didn't take long before her nerves slipped away and she began to just enjoy herself. She'd almost forgotten the fact that people were watching when she stumbled; but the anxious pangs had lessened by that point. It didn't matter; because Gary was there to steady her and stop her falling just like he'd promised.

They danced for a while, the songs becoming slower as the evening went on until they weren't really dancing anymore, just swaying. It was then that Kay caught sight of her reflection again as she rested her head on his shoulder and finally saw what it was that made her uncomfortable.

~~~~

Kay stood nervously at the window, trying to make sure she didn't look suspicious, which in turn she realised probably made her look even more so. She sighed, looking away from her own reflection and staring out into the night instead, something about her reflection making her feel uneasy. Like her reflection knew she wasn't meant to be here and that she was crazy for doing this. Her eyes made contact with Gary's in the glass as he walked back towards her and gave her her drink.

"You're not exactly being inconspicuous, you know?" He smirked down at her, taking a sip and acting completely nonchalant. She envied the way he could slip into this scene without anyone noticing.

Kay mock pouted, trying to relieve some of her nervousness with banter. "I didn't know I was supposed to be inconspicuous. What with us needing to be ready to be a distraction and all."

"True." Gary smiled and moved to put the drinks down, giving Kay a view of the small headset he had on but she only saw it because she knew it was there. That was what she kept telling herself anyway, suddenly more conscious of the small device in her own ear and whether it was visible. "We should put on a show for them, don't you think?" He held out his hand for her to take.

Kay flushed at the thought. "Your plan will fall through if we try. I can't dance to save my life."

He laughed, not at all perturbed by her response. "And? It's not like all the people here are the best dancers. They're all just rich people who come to these events to gossip…and we'll just give them something to gossip about." He took her hand and led her on to the dance floor, amused by the small grimace she wore.

It didn't take long for Kay to forget everything and just enjoy herself, though every so often she would remember what they were doing here as Gary looked around the room to check on security. Even with him leaning in close and pointed out to her that the guests were none the wiser and were watching them closely, trying to figure out who the newcomers were that were stealing the show, the entire act for some reason made her feel sad. She knew that this was his job; that he couldn't let loose in this situation without putting the other members of the group in danger but she wondered if they ever stopped working. The thought of putting them in danger by not paying attention would sober her mood immediately. It was in these moments that she would stumble or mess up the steps but Gary was always there to catch her or encourage her and she didn't know whether that made the situation better or worse.

She felt like more of a hindrance than she had ever felt before.

~~~~

It was a while later before both heard the news that they'd been waiting for but they tried to act as they had been before and continued the dance. Luckily the music had gotten slower and it seemed less suspicious for them to be having a conversation whilst swaying to the beat.

"How did it go?" Gary whispered into the headset, pulling Kay closer to seem like he was whispering to her, glancing up subtly to make sure no one else was near enough to hear while he did so.

It was Ryan who replied. "We're all set here. We're just leaving the building, no-ones stopped us yet."

"Good, we'll meet up with you in a bit so that it doesn't seem suspicious that we're leaving at the same time."

"OK...and Gary?" Ryan's voice paused for a second before continuing as if it was hard to say. "Much as I hate to admit it, this was a good plan. You'll have to tell me how you came up with it later, we've been having trouble with this assignment for weeks-"

Kay stopped listening at that moment, her eyes widening as she stared at herself in the glass, realisation suddenly hitting her.

Reflecting on our own actions can be painful.
A sudden bubble of realisation - the situation you had gotten yourself into; what could have happened if you had just thought things through.

"Kay? Are you OK?" Gary stopped moving, looked down at the girl who had pushed herself partially away from him, her hands grasping his upper arms to keep him there.

"We're being stared at." Kay kept her gaze to the floor, trying to ignore how the whispers rose around them, the stares more pronounced as they stilled in the middle of the dance floor.

Gary blinked owlishly at her, taking a few seconds to process what she meant before looking round, slightly annoyed. "I wouldn't worry, I'm sure it's nothing." He smiled down at her when she looked up, though it was slightly strained. "They might just be complimenting us, you know? Whispering isn't always a bad thing."

Kay sighed, knowing the difference. The whispering may sound the same but the looks were another matter. "They're not and you know it. I-I'm not really welcome here, am I?" She bit her lip, finally taking everything in. Gary's family was rich; the friends she had made had rich enough families that they were invited to these types of event all the time and didn't even bat an eyelid at coming to one unannounced. And what exactly was she against all that? A girl who lived on her own and worked a minimum wage job 9-5 to get by. She looked down at herself, suddenly self-conscious. The dress caught her attention again, the heavy thread drawing her down; how much must all of it have cost? She'd thought about it before but none of them would tell her. Half answers of 'not that much'. But really what was their 'not much' compared to hers? She shivered slightly at the thought before looking back at Gary in his white suit; feeling like a stain against him. She wasn't good enough for this.

"Kay? Kay, listen to me. Please?" He looked frantic, which only hurt her more.

She shook her head. "I'm sorry. I can't..." She pushed away from him. "This isn't right." She bit her lip and ran, ignoring the now even more audible mutterings and Gary's voice ringing behind her.

A few minutes later, Gary stood by the window right where she had stood earlier, their drinks still left discarded. He gave a soft sigh, talking to his reflection. "Well, this wasn't what was meant to happen."

~~~~

Kay stiffened and pulled away slightly from Gary, wondering just what she was doing there at that moment.

"Hey? What's up? You're making people stare." Gary looked around as she stared at the ground, her mind chewing through the newest information it had been given.

"And? That's what they're meant to be doing, isn't it?" Kay continued to stare at the floor, her voice bitter. She tried to put the thoughts away to ponder through later, tried to force herself to act normal. But no matter how much she told herself that the whispers around them were people getting suspicious she couldn't stop herself pulling away from the act. She felt betrayed.

Gary grit his teeth, looking around again, a frown marring his features. "I don't understand, what's up?" He tried to encourage her with a smile, his heart thudding at them falling at the last hurdle. But the thoughts of failure disappeared when she looked up at him, his smile dwindling at the pained look on her face.

Kay sighed. "How long have you had this assignment, Gary?" She counted her breaths as his eyes widened, biting her lip to help keep the tears back, when he caught her drift and confirmed her suspicions. "You knew before we met, didn't you? Was I just part of this plan all along?" She looked down at the floor again, not knowing if she really wanted to hear the answer. She picked at the dress's embroidery again, feeling slightly nauseous as she wondered where they had got the dress from. She shivered, the red flowers blossoming to blood stains before her eyes, her hand darting away from it, almost scared it would transfer onto her skin. What was she doing here? She had just been an accomplice in a crime and for what? The adrenaline that she had been feeling, the excitement she had wanted revealed itself for what it was; stupid and reckless and now she just wanted to run from it all.

"Wait- this is a misunderstanding." Gary tried to keep quiet, his eyes frantically searching her face, trying to get his message across. "At first that's what I had planned but-"

Kay stopped him with a finger to his lip. She shook her head and drew further away from him into the crowd. "Save it. I-I don't want to know." It took her a minute to realise she was running, running from it all in an attempt to pretend it had never happened. She tried not to laugh at herself scornfully as she realised she was making an even bigger diversion for the group. At least they got what they wanted.

Gary turned towards the window, his thoughts scrambling in an attempt to figure out what he had done wrong. What he should have said when he hadn't. What he could have done to prevent this. He looked behind him in the glass, eyes still on him from intrigued guests and decided it was probably time to make an exit even if his thoughts weren't on the job anymore. He muttered quietly into the headset, knowing the others could hear him even if they were staying quiet. "Ryan, maybe you were right after all...I shouldn't have gotten her involved."

Chapter: 6. Lighting

Even when we try our hardest to break away, our reflection stares right back at us.

"Gary?" Kay opened the door to her apartment a crack wider when she realised who it was that had been banging at her door, her eyes wide with confusion. She gave him a quick appraising look, trying not to let her guard down and giggle at his bedraggled state; the weather outside being shown to her without her having to look outside.

He flicked his wet hair out of his face, his expression serious. "Kay, we need to talk."

"If you want the dress back, I already left it at the hideaway." She stared at him dubiously, not expecting there to be anything else for them to talk about. Her mind trailed back to sneaking back into the hideaway only to hear her name being called just as she was leaving. She had run as fast as she could but at least the bag on her back didn't feel like it was weighing her down like it had on the way. Taking the outfit back had felt like she was cutting the strings.

He tutted, trying not to let his frustration show. "I'm not here for some dress, I'm here for you. I don't want you to disappear again."

Kay looked away from him, the look of hope in his eyes hurting her. "You know as well as I do, I don't fit-"

"Of course you do." He stood closer, hoping she would hear him out and not close the door on him. "I won't let anyone choose for us." His eyes were desperate as he scanned her for her reaction. "I don't want you to leave- unless it's completely your choice to leave and not because of what others might think. If that's it, just tell me and I'll go right now."

"I don't want to leave..." She muttered, looking down at her shuffling feet. "But-" She stopped, looking behind him, a noise in the corridor alerting her to another presence.

"What is it?" Gary turned to look behind him, his face changing from one of confusion to disgust. "Ahh."

"Who are they?" She poked her head round the door further to take in the men walking close by.

"Friends...of the family." Gary grimaced before calling out to them. "So, they had me followed? Is this what it's come to?"

One of the men smiled back, ignoring the hostile atmosphere. "Yes but it was so that we could bring you back home. Your family was worried about you coming to…this part of the neighbourhood."

"Of course." Gary sighed before turning back to Kay, pulling her into a swift hug. "I'll sort this out and be back, I promise."

"Actually she's been asked to accompany us."

"What?" Gary's voice was sharp as he turned back to glare at the pair.

The same man shrugged. "Orders are orders sir, and our orders are to escort you and the lady back to the mansion."

"Perfect. Just perfect."

Gary's worried frown and sarcastic comment did nothing to calm Kay's nerves.

~~~~

Kay opened the door to her apartment fully with a sigh, her facial expression a mixture of hurt and annoyance at the man standing before her. "What is it, Gary?" She looked him up and down, an eyebrow quirking up. "You're soaked."

"Yeah, well it is raining outside." Gary tried to smirk, tried to start the banter like they would have before, but it wasn't coming through quite as he'd hoped. "Kay-"

"You want the dress, right?" She tried to turn and get it, having left it hanging behind her mirror. She'd tried to take it back to base but she'd heard someone calling when she'd been there and made a run for it, the dress feeling like a weight against her back as she ran away from them for a second time. Gary tutting caught her attention though and she stayed put, her hands crossing defensively in front of her. *"What?"*

"I don't care about the dress." Gary looked at her agitatedly, trying to figure out what to say and how to start. *"I'm...I'm sorry, OK? I never meant to make you feel...expendable."* He bit his lip as he watched her, hoping for a sign that she understood.

Kay sighed again, looking away. *"Really? So how was I meant to feel, exactly?"*

He tried to catch her eye before continuing, wanting her to realise he was being genuine. *"OK, at first this was what I had intended- wait, hear me out, please."* Gary took a step closer, worried she was about to close the door on him, his hand resting on the frame. *"Please, just let me explain. At first that was what I wanted. But that changed as I got to know you. I've been messed up these last few weeks, I haven't felt right, the base feels so much lonelier without you there. Everyone can feel it. We shouldn't have – I shouldn't have treated you like this."* He raked a hand through his hair, desperate for her understand. *"I don't want you to leave my life like this, I wish I could change the clock back but I promise that from now on you won't have to worry about that part of my life again, really, I swear."*

"How can you say that?" Kay looked away from him again, trying not to get hopeful that this could all work out. That this wasn't just another plan to get her involved again. *"How can you just-"* Movement caught her eye, making her look up again, going silent as she stared behind his shoulder.

Gary blinked at her, confused for a second before turning round. "Oh, it's you." He glared at the two men hovering nearby in the gloom of the hallway.

Kay gulped as she poked her head round the corner, her suspicions confirmed as she took in the two men. "Don't have to worry, huh?" She tried to make light of the situation.

Gary smirked with her, glad that there was still some humour between them. "Yeah, sorry about that." He turned back to the men. "Come to take me back to the boss?"

One grinned. "You know us. And you know the boss; he hasn't taken your quitting lightly."

Gary nodded silently before turning back to Kay, leaning in close to her to speak. "I'll be back, I promise." His eyes however showed his doubt.

"We'll be taking your friend as well." The man grinned again, this time aimed at her, sending a shiver down her spine.

"What? Why? She has nothing to do with this." Gary turned on the pair, making sure Kay was behind him as he shifted, ready for a fight.

The man cocked an eyebrow at him. "Nothing to do with this?" He shrugged at Gary's words. "Whatever, we'll be taking you both back as the boss requested. I'd suggest you came quietly."

Kay stared at Gary; the look of apprehension on his face making her heart beat faster as she wondered just what she had gotten herself into all that time ago when she'd taken the risk and let this man into her life.

Even so, she wasn't sure she'd have it any other way even at this point. He'd been ready to risk everything for her as well.

"I'm so sorry, Kay."

In a car at night we can see our reflection in the window, but against a night sky and endless flickers of light from streetlamps do we really know where we're going if we aren't told?
Familiar streets can suddenly seem unrecognisable in the cover of night.

Kay gulped as she looked out of the window, the streets unrecognisable in between the darkness and the almost blinding flashes from other cars coming the opposite way. She flinched slightly as she felt a touch on her hand, relaxing only when she glanced over at Gary.

He squeezed her hand and smiled, though the smile didn't reach his eyes. "Everything's going to be fine." He whispered before taking her hand in his properly, making sure not to let go; trying to show her she was safe.

"Everything'll be fine..." Kay nodded back at him, mouthing the words back. She bit her lip, her mouth dry before she turned once again to look out the window, hoping to figure out where she was. It never hurt to be prepared for the worst.

~~~~

Kay stared out of the window, trying not to appear too nervous as she sat in the back of a car with absolutely no idea where she was headed. She looked down as she felt Gary's hand wrap around hers on her knee, not until then noticing her leg had been tapping nervously. She looking up at him, her eyes betraying her worry and nervousness.

"Hey, don't look like that. You're just meeting my parents." Gary spoke loudly, squeezing her hand as he did so, not caring what those in front thought of him.

Kay smiled slightly and nodded, squeezing his hand in return and was happy that he didn't let go.

**A reflection can sometimes disappear, depending on the environment.
Sometimes there is too much light.**

Kay squinted as she entered what she guessed was Gary's childhood home. Marble encased the floor and stairways, brightly lit with chandeliers to the point where she couldn't even see herself in the shining marble. She took a second to adjust to the abrupt change in light conditions having just come in from a darkened car.

"So this is her, is it?"

A man glared at her, making her wince slightly though at the same time his demeanour aggravated her. "You should know that already. I was at your big event after all." She bit her tongue, realising she'd said exactly what she was thinking without heeding the possible consequences. Gary trying not to chuckle beside her reassured her that she hadn't done too badly though.

The man stood for a second in shock, obviously not expecting the comeback. He shook his head, ignoring her before turning to his son. "So, what do you have to say for yourself?"

He shrugged, still smiling. "I don't know what you mean, father." He sobered up at the look he got. "I'm not leaving her if that's what you're thinking."

"I don't approve."

"Well, tough. You only disapprove because you're not getting something out of it." Gary stood his ground. "You've already heard what I have to say on the matter when you brought it up before. If you don't like it, disinherit me."

"Gary-" Kay looked at him, shocked at the words he was saying, what he'd do for her. A spark of happiness fizzled through her but at the same time an almost nauseous guilt. "Y-you shouldn't. Not just-"

"Don't." Gary smiled at her, hoping it showed that this was what he wanted. "You said you didn't want to leave, right?" His smile grew when she nodded before he turned back to his father. "So now it's just up to you."

Kay gulped and looked back at his father who at that moment was speechless. She hoped that was him thinking it through and not him about to angrily explode at the pair of them.

Whereas at other times, there is too little light.

Kay shivered as she entered the darkened room. No streetlights shone through the blacked out windows. The only real source of light flickered from a small lamp; illuminating a small circular area that showed her a desk and the figure of a man behind it though she couldn't make out any distinguishing features. A light shone from the open door, behind them so they could see each other but still the man ahead was shrouded in darkness.

"Gary, Gary, what have you gotten yourself into here?" The man moved slightly behind the desk, a soft sigh emanating out of the darkness. "You know that you aren't allowed to add members into your little group without my permission."

"I didn't mean for her to join; I just wanted her input on the one assignment." Gary struggled to find the right words, worry showing on his face. "I only meant for it to be the once-"

The man held up a hand to stop him. "Never the less she knows about your group, what's to stop her going to the police? You are criminals, after all. You should have taken care of her once the assignment was complete." His tone became sharper, his eyes narrowing as it looked like Gary was about to interrupt him. "And then for you to decide to try and leave the syndicate because of this, do you have any idea what you're saying?"

Gary nodded. "I know exactly what I'm saying. And I'm not that much of an idiot to think you'd believe me if I said differently by this point." He looked around at Kay, still holding her hand, his eyes only now showing defeat.

The man sighed. "Quite right, you'd be quite the loose cannon now. It's a shame. You were good at your job. I'll take it I can't change your mind at all?"

Gary nodded. "Sorry, my mind's made up."

"That really is a shame." The man gestured behind him.

A crack of a gunshot sounded throughout the enclosed room, followed by a sickening thud and an echoing scream.

A scream which was silenced by another ringing shot.

Chapter 7: Of Stained Glass...

Through the colours of stained glass, most of the time we can't see our own reflection.

Everything was happening in a rush.

But she wasn't particularly complaining.

Kay stared above her at the intricate images in the churches stain glass windows with a soft nervous smile. She kept wondering what she looked like; whether she looked as frayed as her nerves were at that moment as she fidgeted with the bouquet in her hands.

"Not getting cold feet, are you?" Liam stood behind her, a grin on his face as he helped her with the trail of her dress, making sure she didn't trip over before she went down the aisle.

"I don't know. Are you having cold feet about telling your parents about you and Ryan?" Kay grinned back, getting her own back at the now blushing guy behind her.

"Shut up, we said we were going to tell them after this, you know that." He looked away, slightly worried.

"Alright, I'm sorry. I'm sure everything will work out fine, OK?" Kay smiled at him as he looked back up. "Hell, if it's worked for me and Gary, it'll work for you two." She looked down at herself. "I just can't believe this is really happening."

Before Liam could answer, James poked his head through the door ahead, a bemused expression on his face. "Come on you two, Gary was beginning to fret you'd run off and left him."

"As if." Kay shooed him back out before taking Liam's arm, him having said he'd be honoured to give her away as her family couldn't make it. "Let's get going then." She tried not to shake as the music started and the doors opened, but she became calm again once she saw Gary standing waiting for her.

For all we know our reflection may still be on the other side.

The members of the Stormchasers, minus a member stood in the silent cemetery of the church, staring down at two newly dug graves, almost glad to have a moment of animosity for the sombre affair. The other mourners, not that there had been many, had already left well ahead of the four and no one had asked who they were in relation to the deceased.

"So are we all clear on what's happening now?" James spoke up, having had enough of the silence that had only been punctuated by quiet crying every so often, each of them giving themselves the privacy they needed.

The other three nodded back to him, all getting ready for the first phase of their plan, standing up just that bit straighter at the thought.

Moira gave James's hand a squeeze before turning to Ryan. "Ryan, you never wanted to get involved in any of this in the first place. You don't have to do this if you don't want to." James nodded next to her in approval.

Ryan glared at the two of them, his arm, which had been resting on Liam's still shaking shoulder in a comforting manner, slipping down to the gun at his waist. The truth being told that they always had had the means but not the intent to physically hurt anyone during their heists. A decision that had now altered with the current events. "I'm not letting them get away with what they've done." He turned, the other's following him. "If they think we'll meekly go back to work for the organisation, they've got another thing coming. They'll learn the hard way not to mess with the Stormchasers."

Epilogue: ...and Shattered Mirrors

This story should have ended now, only one reality remains intact.

Kay jumped out of bed, a noise across the room startling her awake.

"What was that?" Gary sat up, hair fluffy and a look of tired confusion across his face as he gripped around her waist.

"I don't know..." Kay turned the light on beside the bed before examining the cause of the noise. "Oh, my mirror broke." She looked over at the curtains billowing in, the cause of the mishap. "That'll teach me to leave the window open." She gave a sigh before sitting down, starting to pick up the pieces.

"Just leave it; we'll do it in the morning." Gary stood up, yawning and came to kneel beside her. "In this light you're bound to cut yourself. You are clumsy, after all." He grinned at her mischievously.

She mock glared at him indignantly before looking back down again, a slight frown on her face as she tilted her head. "That's strange."

"Hmm?"

"Well I know it's obvious, what with the mirror being broken, but our images are really distorted. I can't even tell it's us." Kay moved slightly, trying to tell apart parts of the shattered image before them.

But...

A desolate room gathers dust, the once bright colours fading behind the grey film. A dress hangs behind a full length mirror, completely forgotten.

The mirror slips sideways, knocked by a curtain billowing in from an open window. With no-one there to hear it, it falls with a silent crash.

Inside the mirror's reflective gaze shapes still linger. Flitting shadows dance across. The curtain, the dress's trail and perhaps a flicker of something else.

Who's to tell which mirror image was the real one?

Dedication

To those that we have lost along the way.

I hope that we are on the wrong side of the mirror.

And you are watching us just out of sight.

<u>Author's note</u>

Thanks for reading this far, I hope that you enjoyed this short story! If you did, please check out my other novel A Trail of Cards. It can be found on amazon both as an e-book and in paperback.
K x

A Trail of Cards

Are you ready to play the game?

Shay, a private detective is pulled swiftly into a dwindling police force in a city with an alarmingly ever growing crime rate. A city where people are more likely to trust a gang on the streets for protection than those designed to protect them. But how can he help them deal with cases when there's suspicion and doubt over his skills? When there's an obvious mistrust for getting outsiders involved in their work?

Meanwhile, a vigilante is playing games with the team, making it obvious that he can do their job better than they can with mocking messages left at every criminal he gets to first. But who is this shadowed figure that is running rings around them? And why can't Shay seem to get anything other than cryptic messages when he tries to find out?

Following the trail of cards left behind may not lead to the answers that were expected...